He not only led two kittens away from their mother, but while he was amusing himself in a forbidden catnip bed, they were almost trapped in a burning cellar. Luckily, Hero appeared in the nick of time.

Hero always keeps a firm paw on the situation, even when a circus comes to town and Horrible is carried off by a clown in the circus parade. He always keeps his dignity too—even when he becomes part of the bareback riding act by mistake. He may be a bit pompous at times, but whenever there is an emergency, the other cats are thankful he is in the neighborhood to see that all their problems are settled comfortably.

Boys and girls will enjoy the exciting adventures of Hero and his friends, and we suspect that, when they aren't looking, this is a book that will be chuckled over by cat lovers of all ages. Hero is every inch a gentleman and a cat. As for his friends, their resemblance to any cats living or dead is not purely coincidental.

THE AUTHOR

Hero is Mrs. Dobson's first book. When she is not writing, she takes care of a cat and four kittens, a garden, an old Connecticut farmhouse and a husband. "Not," she adds when telling about it, "necessarily in that order."

THE ARTIST

Admirers of *Hero's* outstanding illustrations may not be surprised to learn that "Terry Gorman" is the pseudonym a well-known artist has chosen in order to experiment with a new style.

HERO
The Biggest Cat in the World

illustrated by TERRY GORMAN

HERO

THE BIGGEST CAT IN THE WORLD

MILLICENT DOBSON

COWARD-MC CANN, INC. NEW YORK 1955

TO THE REAL MRS. QUILTIE

CONTENTS

HERO
The Biggest Cat in the World

1

HERO: THE RESCUE

Hero sat on the marble doorstep of Jeremy James's shop and carefully scanned the street. There were no traveling cats for him to bring home to be fed by Jeremy. There were no kittens old enough to be placed with a good family, and the fish-market cats were behaving themselves. All in all, things were in good order.

Hero proudly twitched his luxuriant whiskers. There weren't many cats who could keep a neighborhood running so smoothly.

It had stormed all day, and wind and rain often caused problems in the cat community. Hero wondered if tonight would bring some emergency. He considered the possibility soberly. When he was a kitten his mother had taught him never to dash headlong into a situation.

There were pools of water on the sidewalks and in the gutters. Hero eyed them distastefully. He disliked getting his feet wet and wished he didn't have to go all the way down and around the water front and back. He would rather have stayed snug and warm in Jeremy's shop.

But the thought of shirking his duty never entered his furry head. Each evening it was his responsibility to see that the neighborhood was taken care of in an orderly fashion, catwise.

A few minutes earlier, Hero had wakened from his nap in Jeremy's shop. He stretched his legs as far as he could, digging his claws in the carpet fastened to his shelf. Hero felt it gave a cat a solid sense of security to feel a well-tacked carpet under his pats. Then there never was a chance of slipping and looking silly. There is nothing a well-brought-up cat dislikes so much as looking silly. Particularly such a tremendously big and dignified cat as Hero.

His shelf was right over Jeremy's workbench and Hero had watched as Jeremy finished putting new soles on the shoes of the little girl who lived down the block. When Jeremy glanced up from his work, Hero had squeezed his green eyes in greeting. Then he had jumped from his shelf, landed lightly among the shoes on the counter, and dropped from there to the floor.

Hero had sat and stared at Jeremy for at least five minutes, and was considering a slight meow when Jeremy hurried to the door to let him out.

Hero had given a quick, thank-you purr as he slipped past Jeremy to sit on the marble step.

He decided there was no use wondering any longer what adventure might be waiting for him. As he left the protection of the doorway, a vagrant gust of wind ruffled his fur and blew it the wrong way. Hero glanced balefully at the thin brightness of the moon coming from behind a cloud. His meow announcing that he was out and around was louder than usual, and his shoulders swung from side to side as he started out in a rolling half trot.

He checked each house in which a cat lived. Going down hill toward the docks, he looked from right to left, seeing that all was in order. A door here, a window there.

The wind was blowing harder along the open street running next to the wharves and Hero walked close to the sheds for protection. He had passed Robinson and Carruther's ropewalk and had started back to the landward side of the street when he heard a faint sound. He stopped and listened, his head to one side, his gray ears, with their long tufts of fur, stiffly erect. The wind was swinging the sign of Robinson and Carruther's with a doleful whine. But that wasn't what Hero heard. The sound was much softer and definitely feline.

Hero could feel the fur on the back of his neck and along his spine stiffen. A cat was in trouble.

Quickly he swung around and started back toward the corner of the building. A narrow alley ran between Robinson and Carruther's and the brick warehouse next door. Hero knew it was the most direct way to the harbor side of the buildings. It was scarcely more than a foot wide, the right size for a cat.

As Hero trotted along he kept his whiskers spread as wide as possible in the alert position. His ears were no longer erect but slanted back slightly. Not as far as they would be if there were immediate danger. Then Hero would fold them close to his head, for a cat's ears are easily torn.

Rain water dripped steadily off the eaves five stories up and dropped into dirty puddles in Hero's path. He trotted on, not swerving to avoid even the deepest ones. He was hardly conscious of the normal cat desire to stop and flip the water from

each wet paw. He was thinking only of what might be ahead.

Hero pictured the gaping holes and loose boards that he knew were in the maze of docks and pilings built out over the water. The docks were no longer used and were in frightful disrepair. To a sure-

footed cat who knew his way, the danger was not too great. But if a stranger should wander through! A shudder went down Hero's spine and rippled off the end of his smooth gray tail. The possibility wasn't pleasant to think about.

Suddenly Hero emerged from the blackness between the buildings. The moon was out, shining down on the harbor from between the clouds, and the wind was still blowing fairly hard.

Turning sharply to the right, Hero stepped carefully onto a small board jutting out over the water, and then stopped to listen. The high building had blocked off all sound and he wanted to locate the weak mew he had heard from the street. For a moment nothing reached his ears except the moan of the wind and the distant, creaking whine of a loose shutter.

Then Hero heard it again, a soft whimpering cry. He had been right. The sound had come from the water and not far from where he stood. Probably over where the tall pilings fell against each other at crazy angles.

Hero answered the call for help with a deep-throated purr-meow ending on a rising note of encouragement. Then he began to make his way over the wet, slippery wood toward the pilings.

Hero knew every board and bulkhead as well as he knew the shelves of Jeremy's shop. But when a loose plank moved and tilted him toward the black water below, he had to dig and hold with his strong claws.

The cries were coming faster now, but to Hero they sounded weaker and muffled by water. Hero ran over places he knew were unsafe, afraid only that he would arrive too late.

At last he reached the pilings. He clung to them with front claws dug firmly into the old wood, and gripped hard with his sturdy hind feet. The muffled mews sounded directly below him as he carefully worked himself around until his green eyes could stare down into the darkness.

Just at that moment a cloud covered the moon and Hero could see nothing below. Impatiently he looked toward the sky. It was only a small cloud and, as he watched, it drifted on and the moon shone again.

Hero permitted himself a small meow of relief and again strained his eyes wide until the big pupils almost blacked out the green.

Suddenly he saw it. There on a floating plank wedged by the current against the pilings, was a little, wet bundle of fur. Only a cat with eyes such as Hero's could have distinguished the water-washed cat from the half-submerged wood.

Once more Hero gave an encouraging meow, but with no inner confidence. The pilings, he knew, were oil soaked and slimy under the best of conditions. But with a rain-water slick over the oil they were impossible for a cat to climb, even under Hero's expert direction.

As he peered down, there was a lull in the waves and he saw the clinging shape more clearly. It wasn't a cat. It was a kitten. A wet, bedraggled little kitten helplessly clutching the plank. A kitten too young, Hero thought, to climb a dry tree with

plenty of good bark, certainly too young to climb a
wet piling.

Hero's whiskers turned down. The situation was
bad. If the kitten moved, she might be spilled into
the water or even go floating out to sea with the tide.

Slowly Hero's whiskers straightened up. It wasn't
a question of could the kitten be saved. The kitten
had to be saved. The question was how.

Carefully Hero examined the pier and the rotten boards nailed to it. He was going to go down
the piling.

His claws were always needle sharp. Now he dug them in. Trying not to think of the swiftly running current below, he let himself down a little at a time.

Suddenly a large sliver of wood gave way, the rotten piling ripped through his outspread claws and he was slipping toward the black water.

Hero dug and tore at the wood. With a snap that almost wrenched his shoulder from its socket, the curved claws of his right front foot gripped and held.

He swung dangling by one paw for what seemed a long time but was actually only a second or two. Then he wrapped his legs around the piling and forced his claws into the wood. He waited a moment to get his breath. The only sign of nervousness from his hair-raising skid was a slight twitching at the end of his tail. Even that stopped as Hero took stock of the situation.

He was only a little above the water. That was where he had intended to be, but not with such abruptness. The plank with the kitten on it was almost within reach. Hero edged himself around until he was just above it and then cautiously reached out a strong, gray paw. For once his huge size and weight were a handicap.

As he leaned on his outstretched paw, the plank sank slowly until almost two inches of water covered it. Then it held. Wedged as it was, it could sink no farther.

Hero put another foot on the plank, then a third and at last he was standing with all four paws secure. Crouching down, he crept forward.

The fur on his stomach dragged through the cold, dirty water. Every nerve was straining toward the kitten huddled just a few feet away. After Hero's startling skid down the piling, she hadn't made a sound. Hero knew that if he made one false step, they'd both be in the water.

At last he covered the final few inches. The kitten waited quietly and didn't try to come toward him and so possibly upset the plank. That showed good judgment and courage in one so young.

Hero's neck arched as he picked her up by the nape of her neck. His mouth was full of salty, oil-scummed water from the kitten's fur. When he lifted her, he realized that she was even younger than he had thought. She was a mere nothing to carry, hanging limply from his jaws, with water dripping from her little string tail.

Afterward, Hero could never remember how he had eased his way along the partly submerged plank, holding his head high to keep the kitten out of the water. But he did. With the kitten in his mouth he dug one claw after another into the piling, and paw by paw he dragged them both up until he carefully laid her on the wharf.

He waited there for a minute to regain his breath. The kitten, never moving from the spot where Hero placed her, looked up at him and mewed. It was a weak little sound of gratefulness.

Hero examined her for the first time in the moonlight. She was so covered with dirt and oil it was hard to tell what color she was. Her fur clung to her sides and her whiskers drooped. She was about the most hopeless bit of kittenhood Hero had ever seen.

Hero licked some of the water from his whiskers and purred a smile at the kitten. Her little pink tongue reached for her whiskers as she tried to imitate him. Although he was anxious to hurry her home to food and warmth, he couldn't help giving her face a quick wash to clean some of the dirt and oil from her eyes and nose.

Then he picked her up again and made his way along the broken planks, through the alley and into Dock Street, where he placed her on the sidewalk.

Hero had leaned down to pick up the kitten when he heard a voice.

"What have you there, Hero?" it asked.

Hero looked toward the shadow formed by the door of Williamson's Restaurant.

"Is that you, Horrible?" he meowed.

A darker spot detached itself from the building and sidled into the moonlight. Horrible walked awkwardly over to Hero and looked down with his one good eye at the kitten.

"Wet, isn't she?" he asked.

Hero nodded. "How long have you been sitting there in the doorway?" he inquired.

Horrible looked sheepish. "Not long," he said. "I was having a little cat nap."

Horrible knew perfectly well that Hero didn't

approve of cats hanging around restaurants. It gave a bad impression. He tried to change the subject by washing busily behind his ear, taking long, slow licks at his paw.

There wasn't much Horrible could do about his appearance. He was as small for a cat as Hero was large. He was black and white, but the white was always grayish and the black never shone. His purr was like a croak and his meow was a cracked wail.

It was no wonder that Mrs. Peabody, the post-mistress, said when she first saw him, "Land sakes, look at that horrible cat."

The name stuck and now Horrible was a little proud of it. It was his only mark of distinction.

Horrible thought Hero was the most wonderful cat in the world. Horrible would do anything for him. But he always seemed to do the things which annoyed Hero most.

With his one good eye Horrible watched Hero's tail. It was beginning to twitch back and forth, a sure sign that Hero was growing impatient.

"Well, not exactly a cat nap," Horrible said

hurriedly. "I had been walking and I happened to see you going by and then you turned in between those tall buildings and I thought I'd wait and see—"

"You were following me again," Hero said. "I've asked you time and again not to follow me. It's embarrassing. Now I must take this kitten home as fast as possible."

"But Hero," Horrible meowed, "I didn't mean any harm. I thought I'd be around to help you in case something happened."

Hero's whiskers twitched as he thought of Horrible being helpful, but he didn't want to hurt Horrible's feelings.

"Then why didn't you follow me into the alley?" he asked.

"In there?" Horrible's meow cracked with dismay. "There might be anything in there. Even a big dog."

"Maybe," Hero agreed gravely. "Then you could have helped me."

Horrible looked at Hero suspiciously to see if he was serious. Not a hair on Hero's face moved.

"Do you really think so, Hero?" Horrible asked anxiously.

"It doesn't matter," Hero answered. "There wasn't any dog and if there had been, well, I rather think he wouldn't have stayed."

"I guess he wouldn't," Horrible agreed.

"Now I must take this little kitten home," Hero said. "I'll get her warm and dry, and Jeremy will give her some cream."

The kitten was huddled in a ball between Hero's front feet. He reached down and picked her up and started for home.

"Sure, sure," Horrible said, trying to keep up with Hero's steady trot. "You'd better get her warm and dry. Where was she? In the water? Was she drowning? Where did she come from?"

Hero, his mouth full of kitten fur, trotted along. He knew Horrible couldn't help asking, even though he couldn't be answered. That was Horrible's way, always anxious but always doing the right thing at the wrong time.

Horrible was going as fast as he could, running and bumping alongside Hero. They were about

halfway to Jeremy's when Horrible started all
four feet going faster than usual and cut ahead
of Hero. Just as he was crossing, he tangled his
feet and before he could straighten out, Hero was
on top of him.

Hero held the kitten up and no harm was done.
He stepped back and Horrible pulled himself together.

"I'm sorry, Hero," he meowed. "I don't know
how it happened. I must have had my right front
paw too far to the left and then my hind paw
came up and . . . no, it couldn't have been that
because my left front paw . . ."

Hero placed the kitten on the sidewalk. "Horrible, why don't you stop that meowing? You don't
know what happened."

"No, I don't," Horrible mewed sadly.

"Well, don't worry about it," Hero said. "It
was time I changed my grip."

Horrible's short, stubby whiskers pointed sky-
ward happily. That was what made him worship
Hero. He always smoothed things over and didn't
make a cat feel so clumsy.

"Come along if you like," Hero invited, "but

don't walk quite so close. Maybe there will be something you can do when we reach the shop."

Horrible knew Hero could do whatever had to be done without any help from him, but it was nice of Hero to ask him. He trotted along happily, careful not to get in Hero's way again.

Soon they were at the door of Jeremy's shop and Hero put the kitten on the marble step. He backed up a little and called just once, a low vibrant purr-meow. In a few seconds the door opened and Jeremy stood silhouetted in the warm light as he peered into the darkness.

"That you, Hero?" he asked in a wavering voice. "You're back soon." He looked down at the step. "Why you've brought friends," he said. He adjusted his glasses and looked more carefully. "Is that you, Horrible?"

Horrible switched his long, skinny tail to indicate good evening.

"And a kitten!" Jeremy's voice rose in pleasure. "But the little thing is all wet. Bring it right in by the fire, Hero," he said anxiously as he stepped aside.

Hero lifted the kitten and carried her to the

box, lined with a pillow, that stood in front of
the potbellied stove. The box was there for visitors
and traveling cats. It was too soft and warm for
Hero. But because traveling cats so seldom had
anything but damp ground on which to sleep, Hero
felt they should have as soft and warm a bed as
possible while they were his guests.

He put the kitten in the middle of the cushion,
then looked at Jeremy. The kitten made little
mewing sounds, the first she had made since they
left the dock.

"What would you say, Hero?" Jeremy asked.
"A little cream? She's too young for anything else,
don't you think?"

Hero blinked his eyes in agreement and Jeremy
padded off toward the small kitchen behind the
shop.

"I'll put the cream on the back of the stove for
a minute or two to take the chill off," Jeremy
called.

Horrible peered at the still-damp bundle of fur.

"She's awful wet and dirty," he meowed. "Was
she in the rain?"

Hero sat beside the box quietly, with his front feet tight together and his tail curled around them.

"In the harbor," he mewed in a murmur, "on a floating board."

"In the harbor!" Horrible's stubby whiskers quivered. "How did you get her out?" His meow cracked with excitement.

Hero deliberately licked a paw, then smoothed his whiskers.

"I went down the piling onto the plank. Then I carried her up the piling to the wharf." Hero spoke calmly in a low mew.

Horrible's one eye shone. "Down the piling and up again! There isn't another cat in the world could have done it!"

Hero's whiskers turned up in a modest smile.

"Possibly," he said. "Although I had a Persian grandfather who was handy with his claws."

Horrible was still gazing at Hero in awe when Jeremy came back with a bowl of lukewarm cream for the kitten and some salmon for Horrible.

"I'll leave the kitten to you," Jeremy said to Hero after he had put down the food. "She'll be in good hands."

While Jeremy was putting out the lights, Hero gently touched the kitten with his paw to show her that she should lap the cream. Horrible went to work on the salmon.

Jeremy had gone upstairs to bed in the little attic room over the shop before they finished, and the only light came from the red glow shining through the check drafts in the stove door.

As soon as the kitten had lapped up her cream, her eyelids started to droop.

"The first thing in the morning," Hero said, "we must give her a good bath. But now she needs a rest."

*   *   *

As the early rays of the sun shone through the front windows of the shop, Hero placed a paw on Horrible's shoulder.

"Wake up," he mewed softly. "Let's see if we can clean some of the harbor dirt off the kitten before Jeremy comes down."

Horrible blinked his one good eye sleepily and mewed agreement.

With a soft purr for a cat so large, Hero woke the sleeping kitten. She opened bright blue eyes,

rolled on her back and stretched and yawned, show-
ing her baby teeth. Then she turned over and went
fast asleep again.

Hero started to wash her carefully, beginning at the tip of her nose.

"What can I do?" Horrible asked.

Hero's whiskers twitched in a smile.

"You do that hind leg," he meowed. "But be careful."

Upstairs they could hear Jeremy moving around, and just before he came down, they finished. Hero realized he had never been so wrong as when he thought the kitten unattractive. Where she had been a dirty gray from the harbor water and grease, she was now a soft, fluffy white. There wasn't a hair in her coat that wasn't pure white. The only contrasting colors were the pink tip of her nose and the pale sky blue of her eyes.

Hero heard Jeremy's tread on the stairs. Slowly Jeremy walked across the shop, adjusting his glasses.

"Let's see this little kitten," he said to Hero. "Pretty sorry looking thing she was last night."

Jeremy leaned over and peered into the box. His bushy eyebrows rose in surprise. He looked at Hero.

"Gracious," he said. "A bit of washing and polishing has certainly made a difference. Why she's . . . she's beautiful," he said. "Most beautiful little kitten I've ever seen." His gnarled hand rubbed his chin. "Might as well call her that. How about it?"

He looked at Hero, who blinked his eyes in agreement.

"Beautiful is her name," Jeremy said.

*   *   *

2

RASCAL: THE FIRE

Hero slipped quietly through the window, carrying Beautiful. She had rested for two days after her terrible experience in the harbor and he felt it was time she went outdoors.

In the little yard back of Jeremy's shop the lilac bush was coming into bloom and the new grass was pale green. There was a patch of sunshine in the corner, close to the fence, where the yard was protected from any breeze which might come by. Hero knew it was a good place for a kitten to play, with no chance of getting into mischief. He would leave Beautiful there in the sun, while he sat on the front doorstep and pondered his problem.

A situation had arisen which needed a lot of thought and Hero knew of no better place or time to think things out than on a clean, marble doorstep early in a fine morning.

As he crossed the yard with Beautiful held lightly in his mouth, he heard a good morning meow from the fence. Without looking up he knew it was Horrible. No other cat, even in the fish market, had a meow like Horrible's.

Hero carefully put Beautiful down and greeted Horrible with a low purr of good morning.

Horrible dropped clumsily from the fence to the lawn.

"She looks pretty, doesn't she?" he asked eagerly as he watched Beautiful roll over onto her back in the grass and wave her tiny pink feet in the air. "She was lucky you came along. Have you found out where she came from or who she is?"

"We never will," Hero mewed softly. "She's too young to tell us. I'm afraid her folks must be terribly upset, but there's nothing we can do but see that she's taken care of here."

Horrible stared thoughtfully at Beautiful. She tapped him with her baby paw twice, then fell all over herself and started to chase her tail. Horrible was happy that she wasn't frightened at his queer looks.

"If you haven't any plans for this morning," Hero said, "you might stay and watch her for a while. I'd like to sit on the step and go over some things in my mind."

"Fine, fine," Horrible meowed eagerly, his voice

cracking up and down the scale because he was so pleased to be able to help. "You haven't anything serious to worry about, have you? I mean, can I do anything?"

Hero licked a paw and carefully smoothed his whiskers. "As a matter of fact I'm very concerned," he mewed. "From my shelf in Jeremy's shop I hear many things. People talk, and although at times my eyes are closed, I'm not asleep. I've learned a great deal that way."

"You must have," Horrible said admiringly.

"But this is something which concerns us all," Hero continued. "Yesterday Mrs. Grimes, who lives in the house with the white shutters, was in the shop with Miss Minerva, the milliner. Mrs. Grimes was complaining about the cats in her yard. She said they were very annoying and she was going to do something about it."

Horrible's eyes widened and his whiskers pointed every which way. "But Hero," he meowed, "what can she do?"

"I don't know," Hero answered. His meow was low. "But we can't let anything happen."

Horrible nodded his head. "We certainly can't."

"It is mainly her own fault," Hero said. "She lets catnip grow wild in her garden. Then she wonders why cats come there."

Hero sighed deeply and stared with calm green eyes into space. He found it difficult to understand people. Sometimes they didn't seem very smart.

"But Hero," Horrible protested, "you've told all the cats to stay away from that place. Time and again you've told them how rolling around in catnip makes them silly and boisterous."

"Of course I have." Hero blinked his eyes. "Do you know what I saw the other day?" His whiskers twitched. "A fish-market cat was in there, rolling around in the catnip and caterwauling hilariously."

"Oh, Hero! I'm sure you sent him home fast."

Hero purred. "Yes, I did. But still, I wouldn't be surprised if that was what upset Mrs. Grimes."

"My! I should think so," Horrible agreed.

"But it's my problem," Hero said. "If you'll watch Beautiful, I'll go out to the doorstep and try to plan something."

"I'll watch her," Horrible meowed. "I'm surely glad I don't have your responsibilities."

As Hero jumped to the fence that ran toward the front of the shop, Horrible settled down to watch Beautiful. A brown and gold butterfly had fluttered down from the lilac bush and Beautiful was making baby leaps at it.

Horrible sat down and wrapped his tail around him, just like Hero. He was determined not to make any foolish mistakes while Hero was gone.

When Hero reached the front of the shop he arranged himself on the white doorstep.

Up the block he noticed Quiltie, the calico cat, mother of two half-grown kittens, Tip and Top. She was watching Mr. Bozzleman, the butcher, take the shutters down from the meat market. Quiltie was a young widow and was doing a fine job of bringing up her fatherless kittens. Some said she was too strict with them, but Hero was old-fashioned enough to believe in the saying: Spare the paw and spoil the kitten.

Down the other way, Hero could see Golden, the yellow tiger who lived with Mr. Summerfield, the grocer. Quiltie and Golden and the other cats in the neighborhood looked to Hero for help in time of trouble. They trusted him to solve the problem of Mrs. Grimes and her catnip. He closed his eyes until they were slits and, enjoying the warmth of the sun on his smooth gray coat, he set his mind to work. . . .

* * *

While Hero thought and thought and thought, Horrible watched Beautiful. He was beginning to feel drowsy in the sun when suddenly he saw a shadow on the grass. It was a cat shadow and Horrible looked up to find a stranger on the fence.

Horrible moved quickly between Beautiful and the newcomer. Then he said a polite, good morning meow. Horrible was badly upset. He knew that Hero made it a point of honor to invite all strange or traveling cats to visit him. But Horrible didn't know whether he should act as host in Hero's absence. Also there was something about the cat on the fence that made Horrible feel nervous.

The stranger answered Horrible's good morning nicely but with an air of casualness. In fact, he had a way of sitting on a fence which Horrible would have loved to be able to imitate. It was gay and racy. He carried one ear a trifle lower than the other and this, with his lean rangy build, gave him a sporty appearance. He made Horrible feel small town.

"Are you a traveling cat?" Horrible meowed.

"I suppose you could call me that, my friend," the stranger said. He touched a striped paw to whiskers already faultlessly groomed. They twitched a trifle as he said easily, "I've certainly traveled some in my time. I'd better introduce myself. My name is Ebenezer. I was named that when I was a kitten. But when I was older, just starting to prowl, everybody called me a rascal. I've been Rascal ever since. Always managed to live up to the name, too."

Horrible wished Hero was here to talk to this sleek stranger. "Have you—have you come far?" he mewed.

"That all depends," Rascal said. "I've been taking it easy the last few days. But originally I came from a town several hundred miles away. Almost a thousand."

"No!" Horrible was impressed.

"Almost." Rascal licked an invisible bit of dust from his right foot. "You wouldn't think to look at me that I was just a country kitten, would you?"

"I certainly wouldn't," Horrible meowed. "I've never been to the country. But I'd love to go. I've never been any place but around these few blocks. Is it true they have so many trees there, you can't see anything else?"

"That's only in the woods," Rascal said. "My friend, the country's quite a place. But I like the city too. I've seen them both. You might say I've been around."

Rascal switched his tail to the other side and then with a quick movement of his feet turned completely around until he was facing the opposite way. He was so fast that Horrible could hardly follow him with his one good eye. The fence top was very narrow and a turn at that speed was remarkable.

"Gracious!" Horrible said. "You can certainly

handle your feet. I don't see how you do that."

"Mighty easy," Rascal purred.

"I don't think there's another cat could do it," Horrible exclaimed. "Except Hero, of course," he added.

"Hero?" Rascal asked in a hard voice. "Who's he?"

"He lives here. He's wonderful. And I think I'd better get him," Horrible finished in a rush and scampered off toward the street. Rascal was too much for him.

Horrible raced around the corner of the shop and up to the doorstep, but Hero wasn't on it. Horrible was in a panic. He didn't want to leave Beautiful alone, but he did think Hero was the one to take care of Rascal.

Quiltie was sitting in front of her house and Horrible decided to ask her where Hero had gone. This took courage, because Horrible knew Quiltie didn't approve of him. She felt he was too untidy to be a good influence on the kittens and she had made it plain that he was to stay away from them.

"Pardon me, Mrs. Quiltie," Horrible meowed louder than he had intended. "Have you seen Hero? It's important, really it is, Mrs. Quiltie."

Quiltie nodded down the street. "If you had looked both ways before you dashed up here," she mewed, "you would have seen him following those two women."

Horrible spun around so quickly he almost fell. Sure enough, there was Hero trotting behind the women. Horrible didn't waste a second. With a quickly meowed thanks to Quiltie he dashed after Hero.

By the time Horrible caught up with Hero he was breathless. Hero could hardly understand what he was saying, but he gathered that Horrible wanted him to come back to Jeremy's.

"Those women," Hero told Horrible as they trotted along, "were discussing Mrs. Grimes and I followed to hear what they had to say.

"It wasn't good, Horrible," Hero continued. "Mrs. Grimes is trying to rouse the neighborhood against all cats. It's a bad situation and something will have to be done about it."

Horrible still hadn't caught his breath but he shook his head understandingly.

When they reached the yard, Rascal was still on the fence and Beautiful was waving her paws at the butterfly.

"Rascal," Horrible said hurriedly, "this is Hero. Hero, this is Rascal." Then he slumped down, relieved that the responsibility was now Hero's.

"Welcome to our cat community," Hero purred. "Would you care to join us? We always try to make strangers welcome here."

"My friend, that's mighty fine of you," Rascal said. "A wayfarer isn't always sure of a welcome." He dropped lightly from the fence to the grass. "Some cats are afraid of travelers," he said with a confident mew.

Hero stretched, reaching way forward with each front foot and then way back with each hind foot. He was always peaceful, but he felt it well to let a stranger know how big he was, particularly a stranger with the swaggering manner of Rascal.

"But I can see," Rascal added, "why you wouldn't be afraid of any cat—or dog either."

Hero sat down and tucked his tail around his paws. "I think I hear Jeremy coming," he said. "He always brings us milk about this time. Will you join us at breakfast?"

"Nothing I'd enjoy more," Rascal said, picking a spot in the sun.

As Rascal spoke, Jeremy appeared in the doorway with a dish of creamy milk.

"Why, I declare," he said, "there's Horrible. And another cat. I don't believe I've ever seen him before, have I, Hero?"

Hero blinked slowly and gave a slight movement of agreement with the tip of his tail.

"I'd better bring another dish," Jeremy said. "This won't go around among three cats and a kitten."

Hero sat quietly, waiting for Jeremy to come back. Out of the corner of his eye he watched Rascal.

Rascal sat very still, hardly moving a whisker, which showed Hero that the stranger had been among nicely trained cats at some time in his life and had learned proper manners.

Hero decided that Rascal had probably met all kinds in his travels and would be equally relaxed and at home either with alley cats or in the bow-on-the-collar, pillow-sleeping set.

Horrible, of course, could hardly wait to eat. His tongue kept slipping out and licking his whiskers.

Jeremy returned with another bowl of milk and set it on the grass near the first one. Then he went back into the shop.

"Horrible," Hero said, "you and Beautiful can share one dish. Rascal and I will take care of the other.

"Remember," Hero mewed quickly, as Horrible started forward, "I said share it. Be sure that Beautiful gets all she needs and a little to grow on."

Horrible stopped suddenly in his dash for the milk and waited for Beautiful to wobble over to the bowl on her unsteady little legs. Hero waited politely until Rascal started lapping before he joined him at the second dish. For a few minutes nothing was said, while the four enjoyed breakfast.

As soon as the dishes were lapped clean they all

licked their right front paws carefully and started to wash their faces and groom their whiskers.

"I understand you've come quite a distance," Hero mewed between washes. "How are conditions on the road these days?"

"Bad," Rascal said, reaching back of his ear with a wet fore paw. "Of course, not for me. I'm an old hand at getting around. I always say that whether the milk comes from a bottle in the city or a cow in the country, I manage to get my share."

Horrible and Hero stopped with their paws in mid-air and stared at Rascal.

"Did you say milk from a cow?" Horrible asked in his cracked meow. "Milk comes from bottles."

"Well now, I can see you chaps have never been in the country," Rascal said. "My friend, everyone knows that milk comes from cows."

Hero quickly went on washing. He had stopped to show that he questioned Rascal's statement. But when Rascal repeated such an absurd remark, Hero didn't want to embarrass him by keeping his paw in the air. Horrible had to put his foot down to keep from falling over in astonishment.

"Milk from cows," he meowed. "Milk comes in bottles from Johnson's Dairy, out on Ridge Road. Every cat knows that, even the fish-market cats."

"No, my friend." Rascal's meow was smoothly positive. "All milk comes from cows. They have a big sack of milk with spigots on it that they carry around with them. When the farmer wants any, he reaches down to those spigots and gets some. Cows are glad to do this favor in return for the food and nice barns the farmers give them."

Horrible looked from Rascal to Hero. He didn't know what to say and he hoped Hero would settle the matter.

"There is only one possible answer," Hero said after a moment's thought. "In the country milk comes from cows, as our traveling friend says. They must be very peculiar-looking creatures, carrying a sack of milk around all the time. However, if that is our guest's story, we won't dispute it, Horrible. But in town, milk most certainly comes in bottles."

"Well, my friend, far be it from me to argue with any cat who invites me to such a fine breakfast,"

Rascal purred blandly. "Shall we let it rest at that?"

Hero blinked agreement.

"Although I would like to add," Rascal said, "that a cow is not the most peculiar creature I've seen. Have either of you chaps ever been to a circus?"

"No," Hero mewed. "Although I've seen the posters on fences and in shop windows."

"Wonderful place, a circus," Rascal assured them in his nasal meow. "Animals, clowns, lights, crowds and excitement all the time. A liberal education for a cat. Take us, for instance. Most natural thing in the world for us to think everybody has four legs and claws and a long tail and a triangular face and whiskers."

"What about dogs?" Horrible croaked.

"Dogs?" Rascal asked. "Every cat knows dogs aren't normal animals."

"Of course they're not," Hero said. "The silly things wag their tails when they're happy. Just the opposite of what they should do. And that noise they make—barking—it's unbelievable."

Horrible looked embarrassed. He knew it wasn't

nice in cat society to mention dogs. He started washing his whiskers to cover his confusion.

"What I meant was," Rascal meowed after they
had dismissed dogs from their minds, "that in a
circus you see animals that look as if they were put
together backward. There's one that has four legs
but otherwise is not like anything you've ever seen
before. His hind legs are higher than a horse and
his front ones are twice that high. And his neck"
—Rascal paused dramatically with his whiskers
spread wide—"his neck is longer than his legs."

Rascal half closed his eyes and looked from Hero
to Horrible to see what effect his story had.

Hero was listening intently, his front feet tight
together and his whiskers at an alert angle.

Horrible was speechless. One ear drooped and
his feet were spread apart to keep him from falling.
At last he was able to meow, "I'll have bad dreams
for a week. There can't be such an animal."

"But definitely there is, my friend," Rascal said.
"What is more, a giraffe has horns."

Horrible's one good eye stared at Rascal.

Hero walked across the grass and sat next to

Horrible, who moved as close to him as he could.

"Make him stop, Hero," he mewed. "Don't let him tell any more fibs like that."

"I must say it sounds unbelievable," Hero agreed. "I'm not sure I'd believe it either, but there was a picture of one on a circus poster Jeremy had in our shop window two years ago. I remember it well. They have brown and yellow spots, don't they?" he asked Rascal.

"That's right," Rascal answered.

"Hero, is he as terrible-looking as Rascal says?" Horrible asked.

"Just about, from the picture."

"My friend, you don't have to worry," Rascal mewed in a confident voice. "They're never let out of the cage."

"Never?" Horrible mewed.

"Never. As a matter of fact there are many others just as odd as a giraffe. There's an elephant and they don't keep him in a cage. He has legs as big around as the trunk of a good-sized tree. His body is about the size of a delivery truck, except that it's round and gray. But his nose is the most curious thing. It looks like a six-foot length of fire hose and he can reach around with it and pick things up and put them in his mouth."

This time it was Hero's turn to open his eyes wide and spread his whiskers. He had never seen a picture of an elephant.

"Yes, sir," Rascal mewed. "A full-sized elephant will weigh as much as three or four big horses."

Hero was still listening, so Rascal went on in his confident meow. "There are always mice around on account of the grain and feed, and of course the elephants are afraid of mice, so they make a cat real welcome."

Hero's whiskers suddenly twitched erect. "Just a minute," he meowed facing Rascal squarely. "Didn't you say those animals weigh as much as three or four horses put together?"

"Yes, my friend, all of that."

"But they're afraid of mice?"

"Everyone knows that." Rascal's meow was condescending. "An elephant breathes through his trunk, you know, and he's afraid a mouse might run up into it."

Hero's tremendous bulk towered over Rascal. His voice was low but it fairly vibrated.

"We made you welcome here," he said, "as we do all traveling cats. We were polite when you told us that nonsense about cows carrying around sacks of milk. But don't think for one minute that we're going to listen to any such tale as this. An animal the size of three horses being afraid of a mouse! It's an insult to our cat sense."

Hero was almost hissing with rage.

Rascal retreated as he saw Hero's back starting to arch and his tail to lash.

"Now wait a minute, my friend," Rascal whined in a singsong meow. "I'm only telling you what I saw. Of course, we'll say no more about it, if you want it that way."

"I do," Hero said through bristling whiskers.

"Whatever you say, my friend." Rascal was very much subdued. "Certainly. We'll forget all about the circus."

"I think that would be wiser," Hero agreed sternly. "When it comes to town this spring perhaps we'll be able to see all these strange animals."

He turned and walked quietly away. A slight twitching of the tip of his tail was the only indication that he was still indignant.

Rascal didn't relax until Hero had vanished around the corner of the house toward the street. Then he set to work to give himself a good washing, hoping it would quiet his nerves. Hero looked almost as big as an elephant when he was angry.

During the talk about the circus and its animals Beautiful had been left to herself. She had grown tired of chasing the butterfly and had started after a fat, black and yellow bumblebee. As she leaped at it, the bee circled around her, buzzing angrily.

"Oh, my gracious," Horrible muttered. "You mustn't do that, Beautiful. He'll sting your nose."

Horrible wished Hero hadn't left at that particular moment. Rascal still made him feel uneasy. But perhaps if I ask him, Horrible thought, he would help me chase away that bee.

"Rascal," he meowed, "look at the kitten."

Rascal had recovered his jaunty spirits. "A pretty picture, my friend," he mewed. "Nothing I like better than to see a kitten playing in the sun. However, I think I'll take a little stroll along this fence. Give our friend Hero a chance to calm down in case he should return soon."

Rascal jumped lightly to the top of the fence, gave a flip to the end of his tail and started off.

He was enjoying the morning sun and thinking how nice it was to have had a breakfast of rich milk, when he came to the yard behind Quiltie's house. There were the two kittens, Tip and Top.

They were older than Beautiful. In fact they were at that age when a kitten is big enough to get into all sorts of mischief. Rascal stopped and seated himself on the fence to watch them play hide-and-seek around the rosebushes.

Tip had just caught Top when he looked up and saw Rascal.

"Hello," Tip mewed.

"Hello to you," Rascal mewed back, giving his tail a friendly little twitch.

"What are you doing?" Top asked.

"Taking a stroll in the morning sun."

"But you're not strolling, you're sitting," Top said and both kittens rolled on the grass and laughed and laughed.

Rascal twisted a whisker in agreement. "You're right," he meowed. "I guess I'd better be going along in order to make good my story about strolling."

"Could we go with you?" Tip mewed. "We'd love to walk on the fence, wouldn't we, Top?"

Top purred with excitement.

"I don't know why not," Rascal said. "Probably do you good to get out of the yard and see the world a bit."

He had hardly finished before the kittens scrambled up the fence post and were beside him.

"Well, kittens, which way shall it be?" Rascal purred.

"This way," Tip and Top said together. "If we go that way, Mamma might see us."

They went along the fence tops, looking into the yards and admiring the flowers.

Rascal was leading the way and they hadn't gone far when he stopped and sniffed the wind.

"Can it be," he purred, "that I smell catnip? I do believe."

He trotted on ahead, leaving the kittens to follow as best they could. In Mrs. Grimes's yard he discovered the patch of lush, green catnip.

There was nothing Rascal liked better than catnip and he jumped into the middle of the patch. By the time the kittens arrived he was rolling around and purring and mewing.

Tip and Top had never been away from home

before and they were beginning to be a little afraid. They thought it very foolish for a full-grown cat to act so much like a kitten. When Rascal started to meow and yowl they were upset. They knew that nice cats never made such noises.

Tip and Top were so embarrassed that they didn't want to watch Rascal. They looked the other way. What seemed to be a gray cloud was coming from the cellar window of Mrs. Grimes's house. The kittens were too young to know it was smoke.

It curled and twisted, then blew across the yards until a whiff of it drifted down and tickled Horrible's nose. He glanced quickly at Beautiful. The bumblebee was still buzzing around but Beautiful had grown tired of chasing it and was playing with a dandelion.

Horrible jumped to the top of the fence to see what was burning and breathed such a nose full of smoke that he sneezed and fell into the next yard. But not before he had seen that the smoke was coming from Mrs. Grimes's house and that Tip and Top were sitting on her fence.

Horrible ran across the flower beds toward the kittens, scrambled up a fence post and suddenly appeared between them.

They arched their backs, put their tails straight up in the air and backed off the fence into Mrs. Grimes's yard. They were on the grass with the smoke from the open cellar window billowing around them.

"Oh me, oh my, meow," Horrible cried. He jumped down and called loudly for the twins to go home. "Get up on the fence," he yowled as he made his way through the smoke toward them. But the kittens were too frightened and confused to understand and they backed away from him toward the open cellar window.

Then they vanished through it into the thick smoke below. The last Horrible saw of Tip and

Top was their front feet grabbing for the window sill and their pink mouths open in terror.

Horrible looked for help. There was only Rascal, who had stopped rollicking in the catnip and was howling on the fence.

"Rascal!" Horrible meowed. "Didn't you see what happened?"

"Funniest thing I ever did see," Rascal yowled. "Vanishing kittens. Here one minute. Gone the next."

Horrible could see he was so hilarious with catnip he didn't understand the kittens were in danger.

There was only one thing for Horrible to do— go down into the smoky cellar and try to bring the kittens out. He shivered with fright from the tip of his nose to the end of his skinny tail. But he went down.

The cellar was black as night. The smoke made Horrible's eyes smart and went up his nose. He could hardly breathe. He bumped into all sorts of things as he went around and around, trying to find Tip and Top.

Then he heard Mrs. Grimes's voice from an upstairs window, shouting at Rascal.

"Get away, you noisy cat. You're making a racket loud enough to reach the next county. Ooooh!" she screamed. "Land sakes alive. Smoke coming from my cellar window!" And she ran to call the fire department.

Down in the cellar, Horrible didn't know what to do. He had meowed as loud as he could but the kittens hadn't answered. He wasn't sure he could make his way back to the window if he did find Tip and Top.

He was about to give up when he heard a firm, loud, purr-meow. There was only one cat with such a vibrant voice. Hero!

The next minute Hero was beside Horrible.

"That you, Horrible?" he meowed.

"Oh, yes, Hero," Horrible mewed. "How did you know I was here?"

"That Rascal. I heard him caterwauling. He sounded as if he'd been in the catnip. I came around to quiet him." Hero spoke in quick, short mews. "He said he thought you were down here.

That is, after I'd buffeted him a bit to make him talk sensibly," Hero added grimly. "Come on, we'll get you out of this."

"But Hero, the kittens," Horrible gasped.

"Kittens!" The fur on Hero's back stood up. "What kittens?"

The smoke was getting into Horrible's lungs and he coughed. "Tip and Top," he mewed. "Leave me—get them, Hero."

"Wait right here," Hero answered. "Put your nose down to the floor and cover it with your paws. Keep the smoke out that way. I'll be back."

Hero's big, gray bulk swung off across the cellar. He meowed, a deep-throated call that carried to the farthest corner. After a moment he heard two little kitteny cries.

Tip and Top had answered because they knew his voice. Ever since they were born he had been Uncle Hero to them.

Hero trotted over quickly and picked up Tip. His green eyes glinted through slitted lids as he found the faint square of the window. Holding Tip, he jumped to the sill. It was only a step or two into the less smoky air of the yard where he dropped Tip on the grass. Then he went back for Top, waiting unafraid for Uncle Hero. Quickly Hero jumped through the window again and placed Top beside Tip.

Hero went back into the smoky darkness for the third time.

"Come on, Horrible," he mewed. "I'll lead the way and give you a helping paw."

But there was no answer. The smoke had overcome Horrible.

Hero grasped him firmly by the neck. Then he located the window and backed away to get a full leap. If he missed, both he and Horrible would crash into the rough stone of the cellar wall.

His long powerful legs drew together and shot him through the air. His head was high to carry Horrible above the sill. Straight for the window he sailed! Then his front feet felt the welcome stone ledge beneath them and he was out the window and onto the lawn.

He turned sharply away from the source of the smoke and dropped Horrible. The jump had been difficult even for Hero and he was breathless.

Horrible lay at his feet, his eyes closed, but Hero could see that he was breathing. The kittens, however, were not where he had left them. They had started to wander toward the catnip bed.

Hero trotted after them, shooing them quickly through the catnip and up onto the fence. Then he started them off in the direction of home.

From the street he could hear the clang, clang of the fire engine bells and the long wail of the sirens as the fire trucks came in answer to Mrs. Grimes's call.

Horrible was stretched out where he would be in the path of the firemen with their hoses and other things. He must be wakened. Hero looked around. Rascal was still on the fence well out of the way but in no condition to be of help. But not more than a few feet away was a watering can. A hasty glance showed it was half full.

It took only a second for Hero to drag Horrible over to it. Then Hero was up on his hind legs with his front feet on the edge of the watering can. A quick push with his hind feet and over it went, sloshing the water all over Horrible.

Some went up his nose and he gave a tremendous sneeze and woke up, bedraggled and confused. "I'm all wet," he meowed. "Somebody threw water on me. Oh. There you are, Hero."

"Yes," Hero mewed, "and you certainly are wet. I'm sorry, Horrible, but I had to do it. You were overcome with smoke."

"Oh, gracious, yes. And the kittens—"

"Don't worry, they're safe," Hero mewed. "Shake yourself off and jump onto the fence. Here come the firemen. We mustn't get in their way and be a nuisance."

Hero waited until Horrible had given himself a good shake. Then they both jumped to the fence and trotted off for Jeremy's, leaving Rascal behind, still giddy with catnip.

When they caught up with Tip and Top, all four hurried along to Hero's yard. There was Beautiful, safe and sound. The bumblebee had buzzed away and she was curled up taking a cat nap.

In a few minutes Quiltie arrived, her tail twitching in anxiety as she looked for the kittens. She purred happily when she found they were safe. Her eyes were round, as Horrible told her of their narrow escape from the cellar.

Hero was modest about it all, but Horrible made it clear how brave and strong Hero had been.

While they were talking, Rascal appeared, looking very pleased with himself.

Horrible stared at him with his whiskers dragging in disapproval. "You know," he meowed, "you caused all this trouble."

"I'm sorry, my friends," Rascal said in his smoothest mew. "Really sorry." He turned to Quiltie. "Is this the mother of these two charming kittens?" he purred.

Quiltie lowered her lashes over her eyes in a gesture that was very becoming to a young widow.

Hero rose to introduce them. Then he turned to Rascal.

"If you intend to spend any time in this neighborhood," he mewed, "you'll have to abide by our rules. One is not to fence walk with kittens unless their mother gives her permission."

"Once again, I'm sorry, my friend," Rascal answered. "As I do intend to stay here, it will be a pleasure to ask Mrs. Quiltie for her permission. I hope she will consider the friendship of a well-traveled cat helpful to her twins."

Quiltie glanced quickly at the dashing set of Rascal's ears and then busied herself washing an already clean white paw.

Hero's gray ears stood up. "Did you say you were going to stay?" he mewed.

"I did, my friend," Rascal assured him. "Outcome of the fire. Mrs. Grimes feels I was helpful in saving her house and possibly the whole block from burning down. I'm to be her cat and all my friends are welcome, too," Rascal finished in a purr.

Hero was the first to offer his congratulations. "Not only am I glad for you," he said, "but it solves a real problem for me. Mrs. Grimes was going to make cat trouble, something we've avoided since I've been here. Now that you're going to live there, I'll hold you personally responsible for keeping all cats out of that catnip bed. Including yourself," Hero added sternly.

"That's understood, my friend," Rascal mewed quickly. "And may I say that rescue of yours today was one of the greatest I've ever seen?"

Hero squeezed his eyes modestly.

"I'll be glad," Rascal continued, "to go along with any regulations you may have. There's not another cat alive I'd say that to, but I'm ready to put my paw and claw at your service."

"Thank you," Hero mewed. "I'm sure we'll all enjoy having you as a neighbor."

Horrible didn't look too pleased but he joined
in the chorus of mews.

"I'd better be getting back," Rascal meowed.
"I'd be happy to have you all come around at
suppertime. I heard Mrs. Grimes say she was going
to open a tall can of salmon."

3.

HORRIBLE: THE CIRCUS

The brightly colored poster with the picture of a big elephant had been put in the window at Jeremy James's shop the day after the fire, long enough ago for this to be circus day. There was no doubt in Hero's mind that today was the day.

He had been hearing the children talk about nothing else. Even Jeremy, who certainly was no longer a child, was a little excited that the weather was fine and sunny.

Hero sat in the window and watched the people going up and down the street. They were doing their errands so that nothing would interfere with their enjoyment of the music and animals and floats and clowns—all the wonderful excitement of the circus parade.

Jeremy was working near the window where he could see everything that was going on and was talking to Hero.

"Circus day," he said, "should always be the brightest day of the year. Once, when I was a boy, it rained on circus day. My, my. Such disappointed children you never did see." He peered at Hero over the top of his glasses. "You were never a boy,

Hero, so I don't expect you understand how important a circus is."

Hero blinked his eyes at Jeremy to let him know that he was listening. He certainly did know how important it was to all his small friends. Any cat who kept his ears open would know. Hero was as glad as Jeremy that the children would have bright weather.

There were others too who were eager for the big day. Rascal, for instance, and of course, Horrible. After hearing more of Rascal's stories, Horrible thought it the most exciting thing in the world that a real circus was coming to town and that he'd be able to see all those strange things with his one good eye. Ever since the poster had appeared in Jeremy's window, Horrible had spent most of his time staring at the picture of Minnie, the elephant.

Never before had the parade passed Jeremy's shop. At first Hero had wondered whether Horrible should watch the parade. Hero hated to think what he might do in the confusion and hubbub that Rascal said there always was at a circus parade.

But Rascal had assured Hero he'd look after Horrible and, of course, Hero would keep a sharp eye on him, too. So they had planned to meet in front of Jeremy's shop and enjoy the excitement.

Hero had already put Beautiful in the back yard where she would be safe and away from the noise. Quiltie had brought the twins to Jeremy's yard too.

"I'll sit on the fence," she told Hero. "Then I can see the parade as it passes the opening between the houses, but still be with the kittens."

Hero wondered why Horrible and Rascal hadn't arrived, but in a few minutes he saw them coming. He went quickly to the screen door and pushed it open. Outside there was a laughing group of children crowding around a man selling red and yellow and green and blue balloons, all different sizes and shapes. Hero swung around them and trotted over to meet his friends.

After the good morning meows were said, both Hero and Rascal sat on the doorstep with their tails curled neatly around their legs. Horrible looked from one to the other.

"Me, oh my, meow," he said. "How can you sit there with your whiskers just so, when you know the circus parade will soon be here? I'm so excited I could yowl."

The tip of Hero's tail flicked in amusement. "Yowling like a fish-market cat won't hurry it any."

Rascal blinked his eyes in agreement. "He hasn't stopped since early morning," he said. "If he wasn't meowing he was mewing, and sometimes he purred. But, my friend, for continuous cat noise, I've never heard better."

Horrible looked downcast. He sat on the step next to Hero. Fortunately for him, they didn't have to wait long.

They soon heard the oompah-oompah of the big bass horn and the shrill notes of the rest of the band. In a few minutes the parade swung around the corner.

The children standing along the curb squealed with delight when they saw Minnie, the elephant, leading the way. Minnie had been with the circus a long time and always walked straight down the middle of the street, swinging her trunk from side to side in the most dignified way. On her back she carried a shining, little red and gold house, and on her head rode a boy dressed in bright blue trousers and silver shoes, with a red cloth wrapped around him like a belt.

Horrible's good eye almost popped out of his head when he saw Minnie. She looked almost as big as a house. Hero didn't squirm around like Horrible, but his green eyes were wide with astonishment.

Behind Minnie came a blue and gold float with the band on it. Horses, all snowy white with riders in fancy dresses of different colors, followed the band. Then came the shiny, bright red circus wagons with animals of all sorts in them. By this time Hero had seen so much that he didn't think there could be anything more to see. But there was. There were the clowns.

Horrible thought they were the most wonderfully amazing people he had ever seen. He ran down from the doorstep and squeezed his way between the legs of the children until he was on the edge of the curb, almost in the street.

Then the funniest clown of all came along. He was dressed in long skirts that kept tangling around his feet and tripping him. He wore a tiny hat with a long feather that curled down in front of his big red nose. He was a very large clown and was pushing a very small doll carriage.

Horrible thought he was so funny that he leaned way over the curb to see better. Just as the clown went by, Horrible slipped off the curb into the gutter.

For a minute he stood there, his feet going in four different directions, his whiskers every which way, and his coat covered with dust. Then the clown reached down and scooped him up.

"Well, well, look who's here," he said. He held Horrible up high in the air. "You're the lucky one. You don't have to put on make-up to be funny, do you?"

Horrible was only a few inches from the clown's face. It was painted white, with a big mouth that went from cheek to cheek and funny eyebrows that went way up in points. For a minute Horrible was frightened. Then he looked into the clown's eyes and saw that he needn't be afraid. All the clown wanted was to have Horrible help him make the children laugh.

"How would you like a ride in my carriage?" the clown asked in a voice loud enough for all the people to hear. Then he settled Horrible in the doll carriage while the children laughed and clapped their hands.

As soon as Horrible realized they were clapping for him, he perked up and sat looking over the side of the carriage, with his whiskers blowing in the wind and his ears all askew. Never before had people given him so much attention.

The clown leaned over. "You're doing fine," he whispered to Horrible. "Just keep it up and we'll make a clown of you yet." Then he pushed the carriage along and there was Horrible, part of the circus parade.

Hero and Rascal watched all this in amazement. It happened so quickly that they hardly had time to think before the parade moved along and Horrible with it. Then another float was passing the shop. A little golden-haired, blue-eyed girl rode on it, holding a black and white cat in her arms, and the children squealed happily, "There's Alice in Wonderland!"

"That cat is Daisy!" Rascal meowed. "I remember her. We've gone mousing together. This must be Ramboletto's Circus and that's Alice, his daughter."

Hero only glanced at Alice and Daisy. He was stretching as far as he could to look around the people and watch Horrible. But all he saw was the clown's broad back going down the street.

"Imagine," Rascal mewed, "seeing Daisy again."

"I'd much rather see Horrible," Hero said flatly. He left the step and started along the sidewalk. "We can't let Horrible go off in the parade alone."

"Oh, he'll be all right," Rascal answered. "My friend, it will be the making of him. There's nothing like a circus."

"You don't know Horrible," Hero mewed over his shoulder. "He's probably trembling on the verge of a cat fit."

It was too bad that Hero couldn't see Horrible. He was standing with his front feet on the edge

of the carriage so that people could see him better.
He had never been happier in his life.

Rascal almost had to run to keep up with Hero.
"If you want to follow Horrible, the thing to do
is catch a ride," he panted. "Let me show you."

Rascal turned and wove his way between the
legs of the crowd out into the street and Hero
followed him. A float was going by and Rascal
vanished under it.

"There's a broad axle under this, my friend,"
he called. "Many's the time I've ridden one."

Hero jumped up beside him and was surprised
to find how much room there was. But he wasn't
sure he should stay.

"I don't think we should do this," he said. He
dug in his claws as they went over a bump. "It's
the sort of thing I've warned kittens against time
and again."

"My friend, I agree," Rascal mewed. "It's very
undignified. But if you follow this parade while
it wanders around town and out to the fair grounds,
you'll be in no condition to find Horrible. Your
pats would be cut to ribbons. It's Horrible you
want, isn't it?"

Hero mewed agreement. Suddenly he sneezed. The axle was not only an undignified perch, it was uncomfortable. The float was pulled by three big, dappled gray horses and their hoofs kicked up a tremendous amount of dust.

Rascal had wrapped one paw around his nose to keep out the dust and his other three feet were holding onto the wooden axle. Hero wasn't sure, but he thought Rascal was laughing at him.

For a moment Hero's tail twitched in annoy-
ance. Then he too covered his nose with one paw
and blinked his eyes at Rascal. Hero couldn't
blame Rascal for being amazed at seeing him
acting like a hobo who rode under freight cars.

It seemed hours before the float creaked to a
halt on the circus grounds. Instead of being a
smooth, shiny gray, Hero was a dusty yellow. Rascal was the same color and when they dropped
to the ground, they shook themselves from nose
to tail, trying to get rid of the dust that had settled
in their fur.

They could hear shouts and calls and orders as
the parade broke up and the circus prepared to
entertain the crowd that had followed it out from
town. Hero saw that they were in some kind of
tent or shelter. No sunshine showed through the
spokes of the big red wheels.

When he poked his nose out from under the
wagon, he was surprised to find that they were in
the main circus tent. Everywhere he looked men
were running about. Some were pulling on ropes,
some were driving stakes into the ground and

others were carrying all sorts of peculiar things that Hero had never seen before. He hadn't known there could be such confusion.

"My friend," Rascal mewed, "here is the most wonderful sight in the world. They run around like that, as if they didn't know what they were doing. But they do. In the end it comes out all right."

He delicately licked a paw and washed his whiskers. "I think I'll be off now. Daisy and I will want to talk about old times."

He stepped through the wagon wheel and vanished around a pile of rope.

Hero sensed that the circus was taking shape under the big white tent. In the center a ring was being formed, and way up around the poles Hero could see that platforms and bars and swings had been hung. All the clutter of things was falling into place, just as Rascal had said it would.

Suddenly there was a creaking noise and the wagon rolled away. Hero found himself sitting on the sawdust under the bright lights with nothing to shelter him. To one side of him rows of red and blue seats stood against the walls of the tent, and on the other was the center ring with two big poles on each side of it.

Until he had found Horrible and decided what to do, Hero thought it wiser not to be seen. He had learned that people are seldom as logical and sensible as cats, and he thought it best not to attract the attention of the circus men.

He made a decision quickly. The seats, he knew, would fill up as soon as the doors opened. The foot of one of the poles was the safest place. Then if anything happened, he could climb the pole in a hurry. With all the ropes and platforms and swings up there, it was a perfect place for a cat to move around.

Fortunately the circus men were too busy to notice him as he jumped over ropes and nets until he was at the foot of the pole. With the big lights on he couldn't very well sit in a shadow, but by staying very still and as close as he could to the pole, Hero hoped he wouldn't be seen.

He hadn't been there more than a few minutes when in came the red-coated band playing a loud and lively march. The flaps of the tent opened and more people than Hero had ever seen before streamed by. The grownups were smiling at each other, and the children were laughing and shouting as they climbed to their seats. It did Hero's heart good to see so many happy people.

For the time being he could do nothing about finding Horrible, so he decided he might as well enjoy the circus from his fine spot in the middle of everything.

When the people were settled in their seats, the flaps at the opposite side of the tent opened and in came Minnie, swinging along on her big, gray legs. All the performers and animals followed her in a parade around the tent.

Suddenly Hero's ears perked up and his eyes brightened. There was the clown who had picked up Horrible. And there was Horrible himself! He was still riding in the doll carriage but now he had a big bow around his neck which made the untidiness of his coat more noticeable. When he leaned out of the carriage, with one ear going one way and the other ear another way, the children screamed with delight.

The parade circled the tent and then went

out the door, taking Horrible with it. A whistle blew, the band played a livelier tune and the beautiful white horses galloped in, their manes flying. Straight toward Hero they came, faster and faster.

With a quick leap, Hero started up the pole and in less time than it takes a cat to blink his eyes, he was halfway to the top. There he came to a board fastened between two ropes like a child's swing. It was just the right size and Hero climbed on and sat down. Up here he had a better view than before.

The white horses had galloped past the foot of the pole and had jumped over the low boards into the ring. In the center a man dressed in a black coat with tails, a high silk hat and a red vest, was giving directions to the horses. They paced in a circle one way, then stopped and swung around. Each time they turned they threw back their heads, and their long manes waved like white plumes.

Then Hero saw Horrible. He and the clown were back in the tent. Horrible was still in the carriage. Every few feet the clown would stop and pick him up so a child in the front row could see him better. Horrible acted as if he'd been in a circus all his life.

In the ring, the horses were still galloping but now a pretty girl in a pink dress with short, shiny skirts was standing next to the ringmaster. As the horses swung by, their broad backs going up and down like a steady seesaw, the girl jumped from the ground and landed on the back of one of them. Then she stood on her hands and did somersaults.

Hero was watching her and didn't notice what was going on at the base of his pole. Some of the circus men were working with the ropes and Hero's swing started to move.

He looked down as the men looked up.

"Hey, Joe!" one of the men said. "Look what's on the lift."

Joe shielded his eyes from the light with his hand.

"What is it?" he asked. "It looks like a cat, but it's too big."

"Of course it's too big," the first man said. "Who ever saw a cat that size?"

Joe looked again. "It certainly does look like a cat, but if it is, it's the biggest cat in the world. We'd better let down the lift and grab him. We can take him to Mr. Rawlings in the menagerie. Maybe he'll want to exhibit him."

The ropes creaked and the swing started down.

If Hero stayed on his board he would be lowered
into the arms of the waiting men and he had
no intention of being taken to Mr. Rawlings in
the menagerie. Gradually the swing came down
until it was about twice the height of a man from
the ground.

Then Hero acted. He faced the broad, white backs of the horses as they galloped. He crouched low and jumped. Gracefully he flew through the air. With perfect timing he landed on the back of the nearest horse. He was careful to land as softly as he could and not to put out his claws.

The horse didn't break his stride. He was trained to keep going evenly and smoothly while

the girl jumped on and off. He did the same for Hero.

Hero's horse was behind the one the girl was on and they had gone about halfway around the ring when the crowd started to applaud. When Hero realized they were clapping for him, he sat very straight with his tail curled just so and his eyes staring ahead. He must be a credit to the act and not spoil it for the pretty girl.

The steady up and down motion wasn't at all unpleasant, and it was nice to ride in front of all the people on such a fine horse. The ringmaster let the horses go around the ring twice before he gave them a signal. Then they swung into the path in front of the seats.

On the way toward the exit Hero and the horses caught up with Horrible in his carriage. Horrible looked up as Hero went by, and meowed wildly at him. He was so excited he almost fell out of the carriage onto the sawdust.

Everyone thought this was part of the show and laughed and clapped and whistled. Hero twitched his whiskers in greeting to Horrible and then the horses swept through the opening into the back-stage tent.

There was more confusion in the backstage tent than there had been in the main one before the show started. It was jammed with clowns, and acrobats and animals.

Beside the door was a cart with six trained seals on it. They were throwing their heads back and barking and slapping their flippers.

As the cart went by, a groom herded the white horses to one side. Hero had never seen seals before and he certainly didn't expect to hear barks from anything but a dog. His big, green eyes stared in amazement and his ears stood up straight as the seals passed him.

Hero was still watching the seals when he heard a familiar sound. He peered over the broad back of his horse and there, close to the edge of the tent, was Rascal.

"I caught your show," Rascal said in his nasal meow. "My friend, it was quite an act."

Hero blinked his appreciation of the compliment.

Rascal gave a quick glance each way through his slanted eyes. "I'd suggest you jump down here," he mewed softly. "There's nothing they'd like better than to have you in the show all the time."

Hero could see the ringmaster pushing his way through the crowd. He appeared to be heading toward Hero. In a twinkling he dropped to the ground beside Rascal.

"My friend," Rascal mewed, "this is one time when that size of yours is a disadvantage. No one could forget it. You'd better come with me. We'll join Daisy."

Rascal slipped under the edge of the tent and Hero followed. They were in a narrow space between towering walls of canvas. Hero could hear the blare of the band off to his right and knew he and Rascal must be skirting the edge of the main tent. In a minute they came to an open space surrounded by the living quarters of the circus people. Rascal didn't hesitate but ran toward one of the brightest and fanciest wagons.

A short flight of steps led to an open door, but instead of going up and in, Rascal ducked under the steps.

"My friend," he said in a low mew, almost a purr, "this is the traveling wagon of the owner of the circus. It is Daisy's home. But before we go in to meet her, there is something I feel you should know."

Rascal had seated himself and Hero could tell from the way he wrapped his tail around his legs that this would be a long story. He decided to give himself a good polish after riding under the wagon. As Rascal talked, Hero licked his fur until he shone from nose to tail.

"Daisy has always lived with the little girl, whose name is really Alice. Daisy rides with her in all the parades. It seems," Rascal mewed, twitching an ear to chase away a fly, "that a few weeks ago Daisy had four kittens. Now, my friend, you know how a mother cat is about kittens. To hear her tell it, they were the most remarkable kittens in the world. Alice thought they were wonderful too. Particularly the all white one."

Hero's paw, which had been cleaning the back of his head, stopped in mid-air. "All white did you say?"

"Exactly, my friend," Rascal mewed. "One of

the kittens was all white and Alice planned to make it her particular pet. Until the kitten disappeared. There was a terrible storm and the circus was nearly washed away. When the storm was over, the white kitten was gone. Now here's the funny thing." Rascal's mew became lower and more confidential. "This all happened a couple of weeks ago but the circus wasn't very far from here. They were right up the river but they didn't follow the river road. They've been wandering around to all the towns in the valley."

Rascal peered out to make sure nobody was listening. "Didn't I hear," he purred, "that you found Beautiful during a storm?"

"Yes," Hero mewed. Their two furry heads were close together. "She was in the river. It was after the storm died down." His green eyes fixed on Rascal sharply. "You didn't mention this to Daisy, did you?"

"My friend," Rascal mewed quietly, "I've told you I've been around. I certainly know better than to get a mother's hopes up about a lost kitten, unless I'm sure."

Hero nodded in approval.

"Apparently Alice is as upset as Daisy," Rascal continued. "She thinks someone may have picked up the kitten to rescue her from the storm. Daisy tells me that in every town they've played, Alice has gone all over, asking about the kitten."

"She must be a very nice little girl," Hero mewed. "Your friend Daisy has taught her cat ways well."

"My friend, they don't come any better than Daisy," Rascal purred. "She's from a long line of English circus cats. Very fine family. I thought you'd better know all this before you met her. It's quite a problem."

"It is," Hero agreed. "But I think Beautiful is the answer."

Hero and Rascal ran out from under the wagon and jumped up the steps to Daisy's quarters. Then Rascal led the way to the box where Daisy's kittens were. He looked around, his eyes quickly adjusting themselves to the dimness.

"That's too bad," he mewed softly. "Daisy isn't here."

They were looking at Daisy's three pretty kittens when they heard a little girl's voice.

"Gracious, aren't you the biggest cat I've ever seen," she said.

Rascal and Hero looked up. Alice had come in while they were admiring the kittens.

"You're the cat that rode the Arabian horse with Madame Mitzi, aren't you?" she asked. "You were wonderful."

Hero blinked his eyes politely.

"I guess you're looking for Daisy," she said. "And Daisy must be hunting for the kitten." Alice looked down at Hero and Rascal sadly. "A great big cat like you," she said to Hero, "could probably help us find Daisy's kitten. I wish you could understand English. Then I could tell you about it."

Hero blinked his eyes. It was too bad people didn't know how well cats understood what was being said.

Alice went to a closet and took out her pink and yellow straw bag. "I'd better go look for her," she said.

Hero mewed quickly to Rascal. "I'll follow Alice and try to think what to do. But I'm worried about Horrible."

"My friend, don't worry," Rascal purred. "He loves being in the circus."

"He can't stay alone in the circus!" Hero's meow was sharp and his eyes blazed. "He needs someone to look after him. I'm leaving this in your hands. You see to it that Horrible is back at Jeremy's before the circus leaves tonight. If you don't, you'd better start traveling again."

Rascal backed away a little. "All right, my friend. Just leave it to me. There's not a cat knows the circus better than I do. I'll get him."

Alice left the wagon and started along the road to town and Hero trotted behind her. Fortunately the circus grounds were not very far out and they soon reached the first houses. Alice went into the nearest dooryard and knocked on the door. It was opened by Mrs. Harris and Alice explained about the lost kitten and asked if Mrs. Harris had heard of anyone in town finding a white kitten.

Mrs. Harris thought a moment. "No," she said finally. "No. I haven't heard of anybody's finding a kitten. But you might stop at the shop of Jeremy James, the cobbler. Mr. James feeds the traveling cats and his shop is a sort of cat center.

I'll walk out with you and show you the way."

While Alice had been talking with Mrs. Harris, Hero had sat by the white picket fence, waiting.

"You go down the road until you come to the church, there, where you see the steeple," Mrs. Harris said. "Then you turn toward the—why, gracious me, look there." She pointed at Hero. "There's that big cat of Jeremy James's sitting right there. They call him Hero."

"However did he get here?" Alice asked. "He was at the circus when I left."

Mrs. Harris nodded wisely. "There's no telling about that cat. I hear he does the smartest things ever."

Hero blinked his green eyes at Mrs. Harris and Alice, then turned and started down the road.

"I do believe," Mrs. Harris said, "that he's on his way home. If you follow . . ."

When Alice was ready to leave, Hero trotted in front of her to show her the way to Jeremy's shop. They went down the road until they came to the church. Then they turned and were soon at the shop.

Alice had looked for her kitten so many times, she was beginning to lose hope. But Hero seemed to be so big and capable that now she was not quite so discouraged. Hero waited on the marble step until she had gone into the shop. Then he quietly walked in after her.

"How do you do, little girl," Jeremy said. "What can I do for you? Oh. There's Hero. Did you come with him?"

"In a way I did. You see, I'm looking for a lost kitten and I stopped and asked at a cottage. The lady there, Mrs. Harris, said I should ask you."

"I know Mrs. Harris," Jeremy said. "A fine woman, although she doesn't have a cat."

"Well," Alice said, "your cat, Hero, led me all the way here."

Jeremy nodded. "I know. He probably heard what you said to Mrs. Harris." He looked at Hero affectionately. "He's not only the biggest cat in the world, but I expect he's one of the smartest. Suppose you tell me about this kitten you've lost."

While Alice was telling Jeremy, Hero slipped

quietly into the back room and through the window into the yard.

Beautiful was sleeping under the tree while Tip and Top played tag. Their mother, Quiltie, was sitting on the back step, with her front feet curled under her and her eyes almost closed as if she were dozing. But she wasn't asleep. She knew what was going on and she was watching the kittens.

As Hero came into the yard, she purred a greeting and opened her eyes wide. Hero quickly mewed a good afternoon and thanked her for looking after Beautiful. Then he sat down beside her and in low meows told her what he had learned at the circus about the lost white kitten.

"Do you think it is Beautiful?" Quiltie mewed when he had finished.

"I'm almost sure," Hero said. "I'm going to take her into the shop and see what happens when Alice sees her."

"Wait a minute." Quiltie's meow was worried. "Where is Daisy, the kitten's mother?"

"I don't know." Hero twitched a whisker in

concern. "Alice said Daisy left the circus in each town to look for the kitten. She's done it ever since the kitten was lost. Once I've settled the question of Beautiful, I'll have to try to find her. There are parts of this town where it isn't safe for a cat like Daisy to wander alone."

Hero trotted across the yard and picked up Beautiful, who gave him a little kitten purr of welcome. He jumped through the window and carried her into the shop. Alice and Jeremy were still talking when Hero leaped lightly to the counter and placed Beautiful in front of them.

"Why, Hero brought Beautiful," Jeremy said in surprise. "This is the kitten I started to tell you about."

"That's Daisy's lost kitten!" Alice cried joyfully and picked up Beautiful and held her in her arms. "I'm sure she is, I couldn't be mistaken, I'd know her anywhere." She looked from Jeremy to Hero. "I'm so happy." She laughed and kissed Beautiful's little pink nose.

Hero watched her carefully. He knew that all white kittens looked very much alike to people and he wanted to be sure there was no mistake. But when he heard Beautiful give a little, contented purr, he knew she was the lost kitten. Beautiful would never have done that for a stranger.

Both Alice and Jeremy were smiling. Alice was sitting in Jeremy's chair and the kitten was in her lap. Everybody was happy.

But Hero still had things to do. He slipped out again and turned down the street toward the docks. As he trotted along, he passed Golden, the cat living with Mr. Summerfield, the grocer, and asked her if she had seen Daisy. Golden closed her eyes and thought a minute, then mewed, no, she hadn't seen any strange cat.

Chops, the cat living with Mr. Bozzleman, the butcher, hadn't seen Daisy, nor had Tar, who shared the watchman's little shack at the warehouse.

As Hero swung along he became more worried. No one had seen Daisy and he was coming closer and closer to the fish market. He hoped she hadn't wandered down there.

When Hero reached the market, he saw none

of the cats around. His whiskers turned down in concern. It was very strange. There was always a cat or two in the neighborhood of the market unless they were all together and up to some mischief.

If they were, Hero knew where to look. Down an alley between two rickety shops was a dingy yard paved with old bricks laid every which way. It was the favorite meeting place of the fish-market cats.

Hero turned into the alley on softly padded feet and reached the end of it without making a sound. Then he jumped around the corner of the building, with his whiskers spread wide and his paws ready for anything.

There was Daisy! She was crouched in a corner surrounded by a ring of fish-market cats, all staring at her with fierce, green eyes. Not one of them was uttering so much as a single meow. No wonder Hero hadn't heard anything and no wonder Daisy looked frightened. There were at least eight battle-scarred bruisers around her.

In one leap, Hero was beside Daisy, facing the

ring. A low, hoarse meow went from whisker to whisker around the circle.

"It's Hero," the fish-market cats hissed to each other. Big as some of the cats were, Hero was bigger. Daisy looked up at him as he stood facing them, his front feet slightly spread and his shoulders hunched.

Now that Hero was glowering at them, the fish-market cats did not stare so fiercely. One of them had to wash back of his ear and another was interested in his right paw. A third thought he heard a bird flying overhead and looked at the sky. Not one of them wanted to look at Hero.

Slowly Hero started forward, followed by Daisy. As he neared the fish-market cats, he rumbled a low growl, deep in his throat. The growl ended in a hiss that shot his whiskers up straight and the fish-market cats turned and ran! Some clawed their way up the fence, others ran down the alley. Two jumped to a window sill and clung.

Hero and Daisy walked slowly down the alley. Hero never looked back, but his ears were alert for the slightest sound. When they reached the

street, Daisy was still trembling and Hero stopped
while she caught her breath.

"My name's Hero," he mewed. "I'm Rascal's
friend." He licked a paw and polished a whisker
to give Daisy more time. "This is a bad neighborhood for you to be in. If you'll come home with
me, you can rest and then we'll see about getting
you back to the circus."

"I don't know what I would have done if you
hadn't come along," Daisy mewed gratefully. "I
didn't know there were cats like that."

"They are bad," Hero agreed.

"But they certainly are afraid of you. You're so
big and strong," Daisy said in a low purr. "They
must know you."

"We've met before," Hero meowed.

In a few minutes Hero and Daisy started toward Jeremy's. Along the way, neighborhood cats
greeted them and meowed a word or two of pleasure that Hero had found Daisy.

When they reached the shop, Hero hesitated a
minute. He turned to Daisy. His green eyes were
very serious.

"You've just had a bad time," he said, "but I think what you're going to find inside will make up for it."

He mewed softly. Jeremy opened the door and as he did, Alice saw Daisy.

"Daisy!" she cried holding up Beautiful. "Look what I've found. Your lost kitten!"

With a loud purr, Daisy jumped into Alice's lap.

Hero's whiskers lifted in pleasure at seeing how happy Daisy and Beautiful were. Beautiful snuggled as close as she could to Daisy, who purred and mewed and washed the kitten's ears and then purred some more.

Alice was telling Daisy that the kitten's name was now Beautiful and how Hero had led her to the shop. But Daisy was so happy to have Beautiful back that she didn't listen very much.

In the corner of the shop, Quiltie half closed her eyes in pleasure and purred steadily as she watched Daisy and Beautiful. Rascal and Horrible were sitting beside her. For once in his life Horrible couldn't either purr or meow. He was too excited.

Hero ran quickly over to them. "Did you have any trouble?" he mewed to Rascal.

"My friend," Rascal meowed, "I know a circus inside out. It was no trouble. Except that he didn't want to come."

Horrible's ears drooped. "I wanted to stay," he managed to mew.

"And live in a cage?" Hero meowed. "And have to perform twice a day?"

Horrible sighed. "I know," he mewed weakly. "You're right, Hero. But it was such fun."

Hero blinked in agreement. It was fun being in a circus. He had liked riding the white horse.

"Now," Jeremy was saying to Alice when Hero looked up, "I think I'd better take you and Daisy and Beautiful back to the circus."

After Jeremy and Alice had left, carrying Daisy and Beautiful in the spare cat basket, Hero turned to Rascal and Horrible.

"I'm going to miss Beautiful," he mewed. "She was such a nice kitten. But I'm certainly glad she's back with her mother and I know Alice will take good care of her."

"I think so, too," Horrible mewed. "But Hero,

let me tell you what happened to me. This clown—
you know, the one who helped me with my act—"

"Horrible," Rascal mewed loudly. "Just a
minute. You've been mewing ever since I found
you at the circus. I can't listen any longer to what
a wonderful actor you are."

"But I just wanted to tell Hero," Horrible insisted.

"I agree with Rascal," Quiltie mewed to Hero. "Before you came in, he didn't stop for a minute. Anyway, I think I'll be going home with the twins. They're still in the yard."

"I'd better go home, too," Rascal said quickly. "Horrible, why don't you come with me? You can tell Hero about it tomorrow."

Hero blinked at Rascal and Quiltie. "It's all

right," he purred. "You two go along. I'll listen to Horrible."

Almost before the others had left, Horrible started to tell Hero about all that had happened to him at the circus. His cracked meow went on and on, but Hero didn't mind. He sat on his shelf with his tail curled around him contentedly.

Beautiful had found her mother and Daisy was happy. Hero was glad to be able to listen to Horrible rather than worry about his traveling all over the country with the circus.

Things had turned out very well. He tucked his front feet under him and began a steady, murmuring purr.

19 80